The Secret Prince

By

Adrian Roderick Emeris Comer

Tom and Dick were best friends who lived next door to each other between their houses was an alleyway that led to the park, and every day after they'd done their homework, they would run up the alleyway and play. They loved to play sports together, but their favorite game was knights. Princes Tom was always the knight and Dick the Prince where they would ride their horses to far-off places. Still, unfortunately, they always had to return home in time for tea. So both boys were looking forward to the school holidays when they could pack some sandwiches and go and play in the park all day, only two days to go.

Their parents knew the boy's favorite game had brought both boys armor and swords as a surprise because they'd done really well at school.

Then Tom and Dick got up one morning and realized it was the first day of the summer holidays both popped their heads out of their bedroom windows and whooped for joy then they ran downstairs to have breakfast and make their sandwiches darted out their doors into the alleyway with their armor on swords in their hands and jumped onto their pretend horses and off they went into the park to start their big quest they'd been planning this quest for weeks it involved riding through the pretend forest and saving a princess on the way they had treasure to find and deer to hunt and if they got lucky even mythical creatures to see they had made a map of sorts but had decided to see where their imaginations would take them. They noticed a little girl crying by the goalposts while riding around the park. Tom and Dick looked at each other, nodded, and rode over to her. They tied their pretend horses up and walked up to her Dick asked her why she was crying. She just looked at them and told them to go away. The boys looked at each other, shrugged their shoulders as if to say, if she doesn't want our help, we'll leave her alone, and got on their horses and rode away as they rode away, they looked back, and she was gone. Tom and Dick realized it was time to go home for tea, so they rode off as quickly as they pretended horses could go promising to see each other the next day same time the same place ready to carry on their quest.

Dick and Tom got up early, ready to set off on another day of adventures as a knight and Prince after breakfast and getting their sandwiches; they rode off into the park on their favorite imaginary horses Dicks was a golden brown with a white mane (called a palomino). Tom was Black and white (called a piebald) wearing armor and swords. As they got to the park, they once again saw the same little girl sitting by the goal post, and Dick suggested they go over and see if she would talk to them today. Tom agrees, so they ride over to the goal post and tie their horses up again. They asked her what was wrong. Still, she just started crying again, saying, you wouldn't understand the boys looked at each other. At the girl saying, try us you never know you've got nothing to lose, she looked at both boys and said I'm a princess Tom started to laugh, see I told you, you wouldn't believe me. Dick looked at the girl and said, "Well, if you're a princess, what are you doing here? well said the little girl, if I walk through those goalposts, I am transported to my kingdom where I am a princess but over here, I'm just an ordinary girl,2 and I'm scared Dick looked at Tom and

said I think I've heard this story before it reminds of that story about a little girl who went through a mirror called Alice and Tom said ooh yes and what about that story your mum read us called the lion the witch and the wardrobe both were good have you read them too is that what's happened to you see I knew you wouldn't believe me said the little girl said the boys looked at each and then at the girl well then prove it they said walk between the goal posts and disappear into your magical kingdom as the girl got up to do just that as she went to walk through a coach pulled by 4 white horses came out of nowhere stopping next to the girl a footman jumped down opened the door of the coach and the girl got in with a thankyou the footman shut the door jumped back onto the coach and it raced away between the goal posts disappearing. The boys looked at the ground where the coach had been then at the space between the goal posts then at each other wide eyed saying WOW did you see that Dick said to Tom, Tom just stood there nodding all of a sudden the park keeper Jake came storming up shouting o

y you two what do you think you're doing get away from there how many times have I told you unless you're playing football stay of my football pitch I've just mowed all that ready for a game on Saturday Tom looked at Jake and started to say what happened when Dick sort of shouted over him saying we're really sorry we weren't thinking we won't do it again and tried running off but Jake started having a go again which was so strange because Jake was usually a very quiet nice man, the boys kept saying sorry while taking small steps backwards as soon as they felt they were far enough away they turned and ran home. When they got home they agreed not to say anything to their parents as they would only say they were making it up but would go back the next day to see if it had really happened.

This morning the boys didn't rush to have breakfast and get their sandwiches for lunch as yesterday had scared and confused them but they both knew they needed to meet up in the alley way to talk about what happened so put on their armor and grabbed their swords and met up to talk about what happened and what they were going to do today. Tom wanted to go back to the park and see if the girl was there and maybe get some answers, Dick who was a much more cautious said no as he didn't want to get transported to some other dimension and never see his family again, Tom found this very funny telling Dick he watched too much television, Dick agreed but also pointed out anything could happen if they went back to the park, Tom agreed but stated that he felt he had to go back it was important but didn't know why. After a lot more talking, they decided to go back but be very cautious and not to go rushing in, they both decided to take their horses in case they needed to make a quick getaway, off they galloped to the park's gates tied up their horses and pecked into the park they could see the goalposts and the pitch and people walking around but nothing that looked out of place, all of a Sudden a voice from behind them asked in a deep voice what are you two up to? startled the boys looked round it was Jake in his flat cap and glasses that made his eyes look big and scary, the boys looked at each other and Tom said we're not doing anything just looking making sure the parks ok to go into, Jake frowned saying what do you mean don't be daft it's just a park, oh err yes we know said Dick it's err a game we're

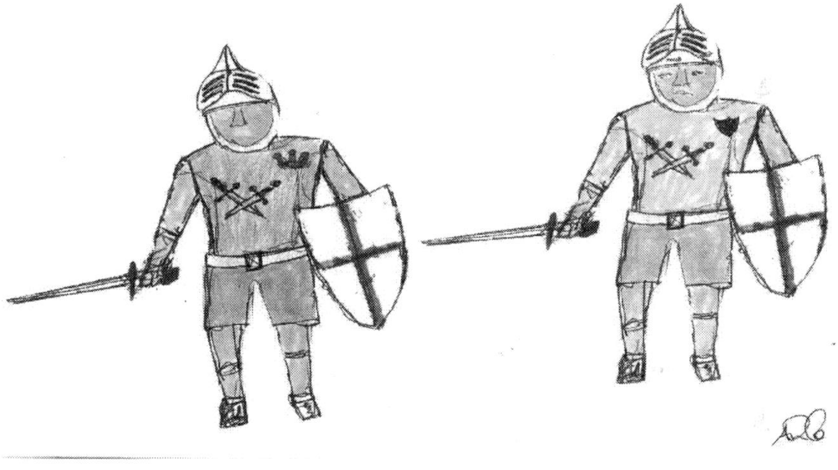

playing, Jake looked at the boys frowning even more telling them I'm keeping my eye on you two I know you're up to something turned and walked away muttering to himself, Phew that was close lets go in sit on the bench near the goalposts and decide what we're going to do now and lets have our sandwiches after all that worrying I'm hungry said Dick.

As they were sitting eating their sandwiches and deciding what to do for the afternoon, they heard a voice say hello from behind and below them, they looked down and behind them asking where did you come from nowhere she said I was already here when you came over didn't you see me both boys looked at each other and then back to the girl both saying simultaneously no. All of a sudden, the coach turned up again this time driven by someone who looked just like Jake the park keeper he shouted at them all three of you jump in quick the boys looked around to see who else was there but realized Jake meant them and the girl, the boys looked at each other shrugged and got in the door slammed and they were galloping off they looked out and saw they were going towards the goalposts Jake said to put their heads in and to hold on as they went through the goalposts it was as if they were swirling round and round without actually going round it was weird but fun.

All of a sudden the coach stopped spinning and as they looked out of the windows all they saw was white but it wasn't snow they were looking at they realized the white was because there was no color anyway at all, Jake jumped down from the front of the coach saying out you get Tom, Dick and Peony, the girl got out and Tom and Dick looked at each other shrugged and said so that's her name funny he didn't call her princess after all that's what she said she was, well we'd better get out before we get shouted at Jake did not look happy back in the park and I'm not sure he looks happy now so the two boys jumped down from the coach and looked around them and as they did they realized that everything was white as far as the eye could see they turned to Jake and realized even the clothes that Jake and the little girl Peony were white too they were sure when they got in coach Jakes clothes had been green and Peony's clothes had been pink and yellow and even their hair which had been brown was now white, Tom and Dick looked at each other and saw that their clothes had remained the same both boys had on blue and white trainers with black trainer socks black shorts Tom had a turquoise T Shirt and Dick had on a yellow T Shirt they looked at Jake and Tom said what on earth is going on have we bumped our heads is this all a dream or I don't know I think I'm scared to find out Dick was nodding his head very frantically while Dick said all of this. Jake looked at both boys and said my name is Prince Jakelm and I am the keeper of the sacred ELM tree and this is my daughter Princess Peony who will one day take my place as the keeper of the sacred ELM if it can be saved and that is where you come in, the two boys looked at each looked back to Jakelm saying who us!, then started laughing, Jakelm said enough in a stern voice and said yes you two.

    Many years ago a strange man visited our realm at the time everything was bright and colorful children laughed and played and the adults were happy he stood where you are and warned that blight was coming to our realm and that this blight would destroy our sacred Elm tree which would

in turn take all color from our lives and that it would take two special boys from beyond that gate to save our ELM and in turn us and this realm he created the gate you came through and sent our King and Queen his Knight Commander and Lady to the realm you came from they are your parents Tom your father is the King and Tom yours is the Knight Commander, the King is my brother and as the second son it is my sacred duty to protect the sacred ELM, I am your Uncle and Peony your cousin I came to see if you were ready for your quest . The boys looked at each other looked around at all the white and the sadness looked back to Jakelm and together said YES.

    Jakelm looked at the boys intently nodded and said come with me we need to find you horses for the journey ahead of you Jakelm led to the stables saying you may pick whichever horse you feel s best for you, Tom and Dick walked into the stables Dick was drawn to a beautiful brown horse with a white mane just like his imaginary horse and Tom was drawn to a beautiful black and white horse like his imaginary horse each horse nudged the boy nearest to them the boys looked to Jakelm saying while we rode our imaginary horses we have never ridden real horses we don't even know how to put saddles and reins on them Jakelm said I will show you how to harness and saddle your horses now but as to learning to ride there is no time for lessons you are going to have to learn as you go along but I have a feeling you will find you already have these skills you just didn't realize it.

    Jakelm then proceeded to show the boys how to harness and saddle their horses and the boys found Jakelm was right it was as if they did know what to do while they were getting their horses ready Peony came in with saddle bags for them saying I have packed you a few things you may need on your journey the boys took them from Peony saying thank you may we ask what's in there Peony said you may but I will not be telling you just know that when you need something check in your bag and you may find it both boys looked at Peony rather puzzled she then shrugged saying I don't know either the man gave them to Dad and told him when the time was right his child would know what to do and say and I did smiling Peony walked to the stable doors opening them for the boys to ride out. Dick and Tom looked at Jakelm asking where they needed to go he told them they would need to ride to the forgotten mountain and that along the way they would have many challenges but that he felt they would succeed, Dick asked where the forgotten mountain was Jakelm admitted he didn't know and that was why it was called the forgotten mountain as everyone had forgotten where it was but suggested that Dick look in his saddle bag that the answer may be there so he did and as he looked there was a map he gasped in surprise showing Tom and Jakelm, Jakelm frowned saying why are you so excited it's just blank piece of paper to which both Dick and Tom replied no its a map showing us the way, they got on their horses and rode out of the stable they looked back to Jakelm and Peony saying we will do our best to fulfil our Quest and return this realm to its former glory to which Jakelm and Peony replied thank you and be safe with Peony saying remember your saddlebags in time of need both boys replied we will and thank you, then rode off along the road with Dick checking the map saying if we go across these fields we will be going in the right direction so they did as they rode along they saw that even the sky was white which made them even more determined to succeed.

As they were riding along quietly talking to each other about everything they'd seen and heard Tom asked Dick do really believe what Jakelm said about our parents and who we are Dick thought long and hard before replying and then said yes, yes I do it would explain our games if you think about it we always played knights on Quests and look at the armour and swords our parents gave us mine has a crest with a crown on it yours has a shield I never really noticed before said Tom but your right,

how do you feel about all of this to which Dick replied you know what I don't care your my best friend and always will be and if I'm going on a quest I couldn't think of a better person to have with me, at that moment both boys looked ahead and saw a large barn in front of them with doors slightly open and from inside someone shouting in a loud booming voice WELL WHAT ARE YOU WAITING FOR COME IN COME IN, the boys looked at each other got off their horses letting the reins drop to the floor knowing instinctively that the horses wouldn't run away and went into the barn where they looked around it was full of well what seemed to be everything and nothing then from the back of the barn came this man he was easily 12 feet tall with a big bushy beard and kind eyes and a big smile on his face WELL,WELL WELL I'VE WAITED ALONG TIME FOR YOU MY NAME IS ARTHUR ABD I KNOW YOU ARE DICK AND TOM WHAT CAN I DO FOR YOU the told him they were on a quest to find the forgotten mountain and that they had a map but no compass, WELL YOU'VE COME TO RIGHT PLACE LET ME SEE I KNOW ITS HERE SOMEWHERE I SAW IT JUST THE OTHER DAY then Arthur started rummaging through everything suddenly booming AHA GOT IT turning round he strode to the boys opening his hand was a tiny compass but as Tom took it from Arthur he realized it only seemed tiny because Arthurs hand was so large Arthur looked at both boys and said THIS IS A SPECIAL COMPASS IT WILL ENABLE YOU TO NOT ONLY GO IN THE RIGHT DIRECTION BUT WILL GIVE WHOEVER IS HOLDING IT THE GIFT OF FINDING THINGS I THINK IT WILL HELP YOU IN YOUR QUEST IT WAS GIVEN TO ME BY A STRANGE MAN WHO TOLD ME OF THIS DAY OH NOT WHEN IT

WOULD BE BUT THAT IT WOULD HAPPEN, chuckling to himself Arthur strode of to the back of the barn and laid down on what the boys realized was a bed of feathers and went to sleep.

The boys left the barn and got back on their horses putting the compass in Tom's saddlebag as Dick had the Map in his they felt it was best to have the things separate so if they lost one, they had the other one. The boys rode on seeing no-one and white all around them after a while Tom looked at Dick saying I'm really hungry and tired do you think we've got much further to go before we can find somewhere to eat and rest it feels as if we've been going for ages, Dick got the map out of his saddlebag and looking saw there was a house just up the road, he showed Tom and suggested they see if they could get food and rest there. As they rode along Dick was looking at the sky he turned to Tom saying have you noticed that although the sky is white it doesn't seem so well white it looks dull, Tom looked up and said you know what your right do you reckon it could be this realms version of a night sky, Dick looked at Tom saying you know what you could be right.

They rode on in silence both lost in their own thoughts when they spied a lovely little cottage ahead and standing in the doorway a little plump old lady with rosy cheeks and a warm smile on her face hello young gentlemen my name is widow Piper, Maris Piper welcome to my home if you take your horses round the back to the barn you will find food and water for them and combs and brushes to groom them, once you've seen to your horses come in the back door to the kitchen and I will feed you as you tell me who you are and what you are doing out here at this time of the night. Dick and Tom said thank you but we don't have any money to pay you with, in which widow Piper replied that is fine you story is payment enough it gets very lonely out here and I do enjoy company. The boys gladly accepted her offer and quickly went around to bam when they'd finished bedding down their horses for what they hoped would be for the night, they went to the back door of widow Pipers and into a warm cozy kitchen and on the table was a plate of chips, roast and mash potatoes and bowls of soup when they looked they realized the soup was potato soup, the boys looked around to see if there was anything to go with the potatoes like sausages or burgers when widow Piper bustled into the kitchen saying Oh I do love potatoes I feel you don't need anything else they are so versatile you could have a different meal every day for a month. Now you two boys tuck in and tell me all about yourselves and where you're travelling to then once you've had your fill and told your tale there's two beds already made up for you upstairs in the spare room, Oh thank you said the boys in unison we are rather tired and wondering where we were going to sleep tonight or at least we think it's night as the sky although white doesn't seem so bright, Oh yes you boys are right this dull white is our night Oh I do so miss the stars in the dark sky they did so sparkle. As the boys ate they explained to widow Piper about their quest to the forgotten mountain and the blight that was effecting the realm and they hoped in fulfilling their quest they would bring back color including the dark sky with stars in it, as they finished their tale and food realizing they'd cleared all the plates both boys gave a big yawn widow piper told them to go to bed as it seemed they'd got another busy day ahead of them, the boys said they would help clear the table and wash and wipe up as their mother had always taught them that it was important to help clean and tidy up after dinner as a thank you to the person who had cooked and then got to bed, which they did, the room looked nice and the beds really cozy they got undressed and into bed and no sooner than they'd said goodnight to each other they were fast asleep.

Next morning the boys got up bright and early and having got washed and dressed went downstairs to find 2 plates of hash browns and cups of tea for breakfast as they finished their breakfast widow Piper came into the kitchen with a bag in her hand saying these are for you for your journey the boys looked in the bag to see half a dozen potatoes in the bag, Widow Piper then said your horses are well rested and saddled ready for your journey hopefully you will be successful in your quest and as you say we will all enjoy this realm in all its beautiful colors, the boys got on their horses putting the bag of potatoes in their saddlebag saying thank you for your hospitality widow Piper to which she replied goodbye and be safe. They both rode off along the road, after a while Dick looked at his map and saw there was a bridge ahead as they got nearer to the bridge there were different signs along the road one said DANGER another DON'T GO ON...TURN BACK Dick and Tom looked at each other frowning Tom said do we go on or do we do as the sign says and turn back Dick replied no we need to cross this bridge it's the only way to get to the forgotten mountain, as they got closer to the bridge they could hear a buzzing noise what on earth is that noise Dick said to Tom, I don't know replied Tom but let's get of the horses and see if we can find out so they did, as they crept towards the bridge they realized there was a giant asleep in some bushes to the side of the bridge he wasn't clean like Arthur and as they watched he turned onto his back and the buzzing got louder the boys realized then that the buzzing they could hear was in actual fact snoring they started to laugh but quickly put their hands over their mouths to cover their laughs as they saw he had only one eye in the center of his head both boys had read enough story's to know he was a Cyclops and in most books Cyclops were not nice and friendly they crept backwards to their horses constantly keeping an eye on the Cyclops, now what do we do said Tom to Dick, we need to get across hat bridge I know said Dick I think we should gallop across as quick as we can and hope he doesn't wake up until we get to the other side where hopefully we will be safe OK let's do that, they got on their horses but as they did the Cyclops woke up he looked all around saying who's there, nobody said Tom of the top of his head Dick looked at him mouthing WHAT THE, Tom shrugged whispering I know I'm sorry it just came out, the Cyclops said oh that's alright then what wait what do you mean nobody's having me on of course somebody's there or you wouldn't have said nobody or is it that your name my names Garlik he Said what are you doing there can't you read it says DANGER DON'T GO ON TURN BACK on my signs so why didn't you well said Dick you see we are on a quest to rid this realm

of the blight and to do that we need to get to the forgotten mountain and the only way we can get there is to go over this bridge the Cyclops started laughing and wheezing saying and that is why you will never cross I don't want the blight gone and color brought to this realm so go back where you came from NO shouted Dick and Tom we are going across and you can't stop us and started to rush galloped with their shields up and swords out as they got near Garlik he swung his club at Tom who was in front knocking Toms shield out of his hand and Tom off his horse Dick rode in front of Tom to protect him from any more onslaught from Garlik's club as he did Garlic knocked Dick off his horse dislodging the saddle bag off his horse making it open and spill out some of the potatoes, just then something dark flew past then distracting Garlik as the boys too looked up they saw it was a Griffin while Garlik was still looking up Tom picked up a potato and threw it at the Cyclops it hit him in the eye and went splat turning into an eye patch the Cyclops tried pulling it off but the more he tried the harder it stuck he started bellowing and shouting I'm blind help I can't see stumbling all over the place, when the boys got to the other side of the bridge Tom shouted if you sit down where you are and think about all the bad things you've done and then say sorry for each and every one and promise to never do them or anything else bad and mean it maybe the patch will come off BUT and this is a big BUT you've got to mean every sorry or it won't work, and the boys rode off.

Up the road the boys came to a forest it was beautiful looking like a winter wonderland scene on a Christmas card as everything was white the trees grass and ferns but it wasn't because they were covered in snow. As they travelled into the forest it grew dark as it was so dense it blocked out all the light, as the neared the center of the forest there was a clearing and in the clearing was a very, very tall tree with a large nest at the top and looking over the side of the nest down at them was a very large eagle, hello my name is Dandy-Lion who are you, the boys said we're Dick and Tom are you who flew over distracting the Cyclops for us yes said Dandy-Lion well thank you said Dick do you want to come down so we don't need to keep shouting up to you Oh yes good idea here I come, and she arose spread her wings and then flew into the sky soaring above the clouds before she swooped down landing by the boys she was beautiful with a magnificent lions body the head and wings of an eagle, again hello I know I don't need to tell you that I'm a Griffin I've been watching you for some time with my eagle eyes because I noticed you still have color how come? Well said Dick we came through a magical tunnel from another place and we've been told we need to go on a quest to the forgotten mountain to cure the blight and bring color back to this realm AHH so you are the ones said Dandy-Lion I have been waiting for you for a long time, why is your armor and sword plastic? Tom said well you see this is what we came through with and we weren't given metal armor or swords to replace it, Oh dear well that's not going to protect you from the guardian of the gate leading to the mountain who unfortunately is not a good being you will need to have metal Armor and swords and thankfully I can help you with that touch your swords and shields against your body armor, both boys did as she said and then Daisy-Lion placed her beak first on Dick then On Toms armor when they looked down everything that had been plastic was now made of metal Daisy-Lion looked at the boys smiling saying and it's not just any metal its tungsten the strongest metal Oh my goodness we've got proper armor and swords and shields thank you so much Daisy-Lion how can we ever repay you to which Daisy-Lion replied by completing your quest but I must warn you this blight is made of magic and will take a special kind of magic to defeat it but I know you have the heart and bravery to win you just need to believe in yourselves, now I must go as I have completed the task set for me by the stranger but know that I am watching over you even when you can't see me.

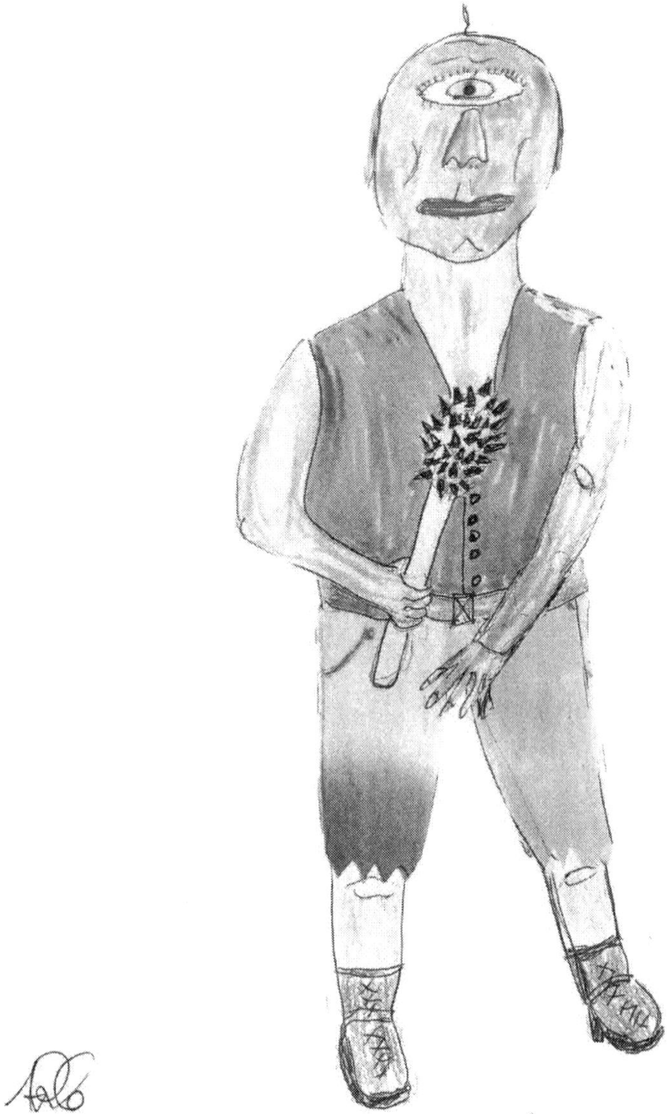

Dick and Tom rode on quietly deep in thought until they came out of the forest, as they did they looked up and realized that the sky was getting dull, Dick looked at Tom saying I think it's nearly night time looking at the color of the sky and we need to look for shelter for the night, Tom looked up and agreed with Dick hopefully we can find somewhere we can get food too as I'm hungry, well let's look at the map and see if that will help, so they took out the map but as they went to unfold it they looked up and there in front of them was an old mansion house hey where did that come from it wasn't there just now said Tom, Dick shrugged saying I don't know as he put the map away but let's go and explore hopefully someone will be there and able to tell us more about our quest, they got of their horses and started to explore as they went around to the back of the mansion they could hear a guitar being played and someone singing along to it, they crept along and as they turned the corner they saw a small man with a big belly sitting on a log around a camp fire strumming a guitar, singing about Knights and daring deeds, as the boys crept nearer they could hear the words and realized he was singing about them and all that had happened to them up till this point as he got to the part of the song that said they'd turned the corner of the house he stopped playing the guitar and singing, turned to the boys and said why hello there you made it then my name is Sparagus and I am the teller of tales in music for all to listen to, Dick and Tom looked at each other then back to Sparagus saying err good evening how do you know what's happened up till now, to which Sparagus replied a little birdie told me chuckling to himself he said why don't you boys come sit down with me and have something to eat and after rest for the night, Sparagus got up waddling on his short legs over to a cook pot over the camp fire out of nowhere two bowls appeared in his hand and filled them up when he went back to where the boys were sitting he handed each boy a bowl and when they looked inside they realized it was porridge Sparagus handed them each a spoon saying now tuck in boys it's exactly as you like it while I go and see to the horses for you. Tom and Dick tucked into their porridge Tom looked at Dick saying just as I like it made with water and salt eh! What do you mean water and salt don't you mean milk and sugar? you know I hate the way you like your porridge and this is perfect Tom started laughing saying we should have known it would be perfect for each of us after all this is a magical realm, as they finished eating Sparagus returned with two sleeping bags handing one to each boy he said now you settle down in these by the fire and I will watch over you, Sparagus then picked up his guitar and started playing humming along to whatever tune it was he was playing as the boys listened they felt their eyelids getting heavy and the next thing they knew Sparagus was shaking them saying good morning boys here's some breakfast for you as he handed each of them a bowl of porridge now eat up as you have a journey ahead of you and you will need all your strength and wits about you, while you were sleeping I took the liberty of polishing your swords with oats from my cook pot I think you will find it has given them a power to help you in your next test. Now I know your quest is to bring back color to this realm but until now you haven't known who you are up against, now it is my task to tell you as you eat your porridge and as they did Sparagus proceeded to tell them the story of how color was taken from the Realm.

Well the story starts with a beautiful woman visiting us after the stranger left she told us she was a sent by him to safeguard our realm and to show us how to protect it, she said we would need to find a special cave and that once we have found it she would live in it thus protecting the magic well we found that cave it was hidden in what is now called the forgotten mountain, and she took up residence there but once she had, we found that slowly color was leaving us so I was sent to find her to tell her of our plight, now I have to tell you at this time I was an ordinary man with ordinary looks who travelled the realm telling my stories with my music in fact I was famous for it and

everyone loved me, well I found her in the cave but as I tried to tell her what was happening she started laughing changing before my eyes, her body started sprouting thirteen long hairy legs and her head became triangular she still had two eyes a nose and mouth but the mouth was now turned up in maniacal smile as she said my name is Comosum and I am here to destroy this realm taking all the magic with me and you can't stop me to which I told her I would tell everyone of what she had done and with everyone together we would defeat her, she just started laughing looked at me saying and who would listen to you now story teller and then she made me look in a mirror and I saw what you see before you now and she was right when I tried to tell the people they all laughed at me so I decided to stay here and wait for you because I knew what she didn't and that was you would listen to me and save our realm. Now the other thing I must tell you is that I know the real name of the forgotten mountain and the cave Comosum now resides in leaching our land of its magic but once I have told you, you must promise me not to say it again until she is defeated because the name is the final magic and once she has she will destroy us and we will be no more that is why it became the forgotten mountain so we could hopefully keep the last of our magic , the boys looked at each turned back to Sparagus saying we promise on our honor as knights, so Sparagus lent in between the boys whispering Emeris.

    Now go your horses are ready it is time for you to continue on your quest but remember what I said never repeat the name, the boys got on the horses saying thank you for the food and story and we promise, goodbye and take care of yourself, but as they go to ride off the horses suddenly sprout wings and fly into the air, Wow what on earth is happening says Dick, Tom just starts laughing in excitement this is great they're Pegasus flying horses, at that moment Toms Pegasus looks round to him and says yes your right oh and we can talk too, Dick says but how? To which Dicks Pegasus looks around at him and says the Porridge Sparagus fed us was magical we are no longer just horses we are now Pegasus and we have the ability to speak you will need this in the future but for now let us fly you to the next part of your quest.

They fly through the air until they come to a small mountain with a Mesa (Flat area at top of a mountain) at the top surrounded by clouds the Pegasus landed and the boys got off, as they stood there looking around they were suddenly joined by what they thought was a small pony but as it closer to them they realized it was a baby unicorn oh my goodness said Tom she's so pretty or at least I think it's a she, she's all glittery and her coat looks like a rainbow of pastel colors and her mane is bright yellow and pink that's what makes me think it's a girl unicorn, at that moment the unicorn came right up to the boys saying hello Dick, Tom my name is Princess Tina and as you can guess by my name you are right Tom I'm a girl only the female unicorns are such bright pastel colors like pink, sky blue all the males are vibrant colors like red, dark blue, etc., I am the daughter of the Royal family of unicorns and I have been sent to lead you over the rainbow to meet my mother Queen Tula but first I need to speak to my cousins the Pegasus, as Tina trotted over to them both Pegasus bent a front leg to her saying your highness we are at your command, Tina said hello Bailey to Dicks mount and then turning to Toms mount and hello to you too Chequers, as you know you are unable to come with us so I need you both to wait here we won't be long for as you know where I am taking them time runs differently, both Pegasus said as you wish your Highness, Princess then turned back to Dick and Tom saying please put your hands on me and don't let go whatever happens are you ready, yes said both boys then put their hands on Princess Tina as they did a rainbow appeared but as soon as they took their hands off it disappeared WOW said Dick that's awesome, Princess Tina looked at both boys hurry up put your hands on me and keep them there

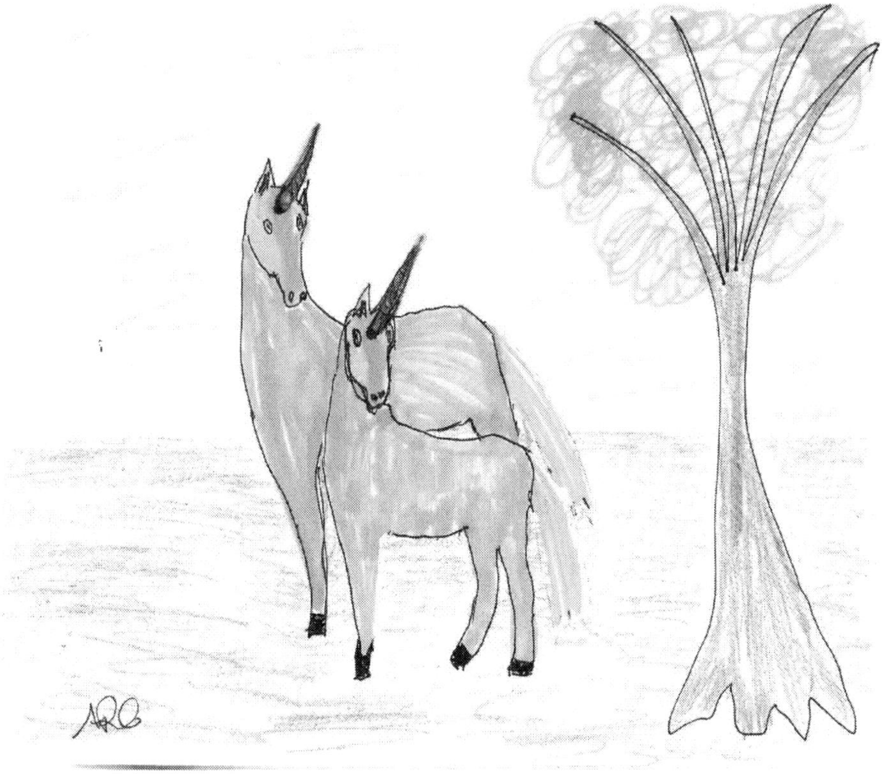

this time, so they did, the rainbow appeared again and then all of sudden they standing in a field of grass full of unicorns and as the boys looked around they realized the grass was green and the trees surrounding the field were also green OH my goodness how IT'S GREEN I thought all the color had been taken. A magnificent unicorn came towards the boys as all the other unicorns bowed the front leg to it saying HAIL QUEEN TULA Princess Tina went bounding up to her suddenly skidding to a halt bowing saying OOPs sorry mummy double oops Queen mummy double, double oops Queen Tula , smiling Queen Tula said that's alright my darling I understand it's not easy to remember, now introduce me to Prince Dick and Knight Commander Tom as Princess Tina turned to the boys they both bowed at the waist saying Your Majesty, Queen Tula said up and follow me we have a lot to talk about and I'm sure you have many questions for you which I will try and answer as best as I can. Now Tina go and find your friends it is time for lessons oh mum but I want to hear too said Princess Tina, Queen Tula replied no my darling this is for the boys only now off with you and don't upset your teacher. Queen Tula then looked at the boys saying now follow me leading the boys to a quiet corner of the field where she looked at Tom saying please Kneel, as Tom started to kneel so Dick did too Queen Tula said no Prince Dick not you just Knight Tom, Queen Tula's horn was a rainbow of every color all the pastels all the vibrant colors mixed together and as she touched her horn to Toms forehead he felt a as if he'd been hit with a bright light in his head and then as if his head was full of colors so bright it made him gasp in shock what's happening exclaimed Tom to which Queen Tula said I am freeing you from the grasp of the evil that Comosum planted in you as part of her bid to destroy this realm she thought she'd planted it in Prince Dick, but as you know you were born on the same day and as you both lay side by side in the cot she mistook you for him thus weakening the spell allowing me to hide all the unicorns in this valley keeping the last of the magic safe ready to anoint you with the power to defeat Comosum, what would of happened if she hadn't got us confused said Dick to which Queen Tula said we wouldn't be here now for mixing your magic with hers would have destroyed us all, but I don't understand Sparagus said he was the only one who knew who she really is said Prince Dick, ah yes unfortunately to keep this pocket of magic safe he could not know of our existence for when Comosum spelled him she made it that she could hear all his story's as he told them said Queen Tula, but does that mean she knows we are coming and that we know the real name of the forgotten mountain and the name of the cave she's in said Prince Dick, no because before I hid I put a spell of protection on the name and the only time he could utter it was to you and only you and Knight Tom could hear it anyone else would hear forgotten mountain that is how it became known as that said Queen Tula, wow this is just so well amazing is the only way I can describe all of this said Prince Dick, well I' glad it was me and not you said Knight Tom getting up from his knees and thank you Queen Tula for taking Comosums dark magic out of me now I feel as if we really can defeat her I think part of her magic was to make me doubt myself doubt us. Now I must call my Daughter for she needs to take you back to your Pegasus said Queen Tula, she shut her eyes and as the boys looked around they saw Princess Tula trotting towards them you called mummy she said, Queen Tula smiled saying I did you need to take the Prince and his knight back to their Pegasus and then return here immediately no dawdling do you hear me young lady, yes mummy said Princess Tina with a sigh it's no fun being a young unicorn I can't wait to grow up. Right Dick Tom can I call you that you can call me Tina after all we're all royal well technically you're not Tom but as the one who mum touched with her magic it kind of makes you royal like Dick and me, the boys chuckled and Dick said of course you can after all using all our titles makes for long conversations, right well place your hands on me and I'll take you back said Tina, so both boys did and again a rainbow appeared and then they were back on top of the mountain with their Pegasus they took their hands off Tina she turned to the Pegasus saying Queen Tula says you know what to do they both bowed their heads saying we do your highness then she turned to Dick and Tom saying well I must hurry home so I will say goodbye and see you at the end of your quest turned and walked away as she disappeared into the clouds Dick and Tom said goodbye.

After Tina left the two boys sat down on the floor to catch their breathes after everything that they'd been told and happened to them they were feeling overwhelmed they talked for ages sometimes Bailey and Chequers joining in after all they had been with the boys right from the beginning, after much talking everyone agreed the sky was getting duller again and everyone was starting to get hungry so it was time to set off to the next part of their quest. Dick got the map out placing it on the floor and Tom got the compass out placing it on the map as the compass landed on the map the needle started spinning madly all of a sudden the arrow stopped pointing to the north and when they looked at the map that too was pointing to go north when they checked what was in the north they saw it was a beach. They jumped on Bailey and Chequers after putting the map and compass back in the saddlebags grabbing the reins saying off we go you saw the map and I heard Tina say to you that you knew what to do next so off we go. Bailey and Chequers flew off soaring into the sky everyone shouting WOOWEE and laughing, all of a sudden both Pegasus started falling in a spiral from the sky both boys hung onto the reins tightly shouting WHAT'S HAPPENING don't worry said Bailey you are safe this is all part of the journey. The Pegasus landed on what looked like a beach they jumped of the Pegasus quickly exclaiming what happened but as they looked at the Pegasus they saw their wings disappearing into their backs are you alright said Tom, Chequers looked round saying yes this is as it should be we no longer need our wings, we have retained our ability to talk and will never lose that it is the gift to us from the realm for helping you.

As all of this was going on a man in brightly colored shorts and a surf board under his arm walked out of the sea dripping wet coming up to them saying Hey man what you doing aren't you hot in all that metal you need to get out of it and come surfing with me you need to chill enjoy stop worrying it's not good for you come with me I've got a beach cabin just round that bend you can leave all that metal and spare shorts and board that you can borrow, err what about our horses said Tom oh bring them I've got some goats they can keep company said the man, okay but can we ask your name before we come with you said Dick, eh oh yes my name is Andysurf now come along before I change my mind, the boys followed Andysurf leading their horses behind them as they walked they asked Andysurf if it was possible to get something to eat and maybe somewhere to sleep,

Andysurf replied oh yea course actually its getting too late to surf now and the waves aren't the best but come morning whooee now then we'll have the waves and I can show you what you've been missing all this time, now come on lets go and get the food and find somewhere for you to rest your heads till the morning and the perfect seas. As they came to cabin   stood his board in the sand and went in the boys took their horses around to the back took off their saddles giving them food and settling them in with the goats as Andysurf had suggested Bailey weren't too pleased as the goats were a bit smelly but decided it would be nice to rest as all that flying had worn them out, Dick and Tom said goodnight went back round to the front of the cabin and went in, as they entered Andysurf was cooking some fish for tea turning he said right take off all that metal the shorts are in the back room for you to change into, oh alright said Dick and they both went into the back room, Tom whispered to Dick I'm a bit worried it's as if Andysurf doesn't realize what's happening or doesn't want to know, I know said Dick what we'll do is talk to him as we eat telling him our story and see what he says, come on let's do what he said I'm hungry and I'm tired and maybe we can get some

answers. The boys left the back room going into the front room on the coffee table surrounded with cushions were plates of fish the boys and Andysurf sat down and tucked into the fish as they ate the boys told Andysurf all about their quest and all that had happened to them as they finished their meal they finished their tale, Andysurf looked at both boys saying well that was a good tale to help our food go down but we need to be up early for the good surf so off to bed for us all, he yawned stretched and got up pointing to the cushions saying you boys can sleep there walking into the back room saying goodnight and surf dreams for you. Dick and Tom looked at each other and Dick said well that went well, not, I know said Tom but what do we do now, well said Dick I think we'll do as Andysurf said and go to sleep by the looks of it we've got an early start in the morning, and with that Dick and Tom laid down and went to sleep.

What seemed like only minutes later they Heard Andysurf shouting come on dudes surfs up as he ran out the door grabbing his surfboard grab yours and I'll teach you how it's done the waves are perfect this morning, the boys jumped up ran out after Andysurf grabbing a surf board each running to catch up to Andysurf. When they got to the water's edge Andysurf was waiting for them, he told them to lay their boards on the sand laying on their stomachs on them and pretend to paddle with their hands and once they felt ready to jump up placing one foot at the front of the board and one at the back once they had practiced the manoeuvres a few times Andysurf said they were ready to try doing it in the water cresting on the waves. The boys grabbed their boards off the sand and followed Andysurf into the water once they were in deep enough water they did all that Andysurf had told them to do, they spent hours out in the water going back and forth whooping and hollering having a great time. After a time Andysurf said the waves were no longer any good and that it was time to return to the cabin get dressed as they needed to talk.

Once everybody was dressed the boys back in their armor Andysurf turned to the boys saying whilst surfing I was thinking about your tale and I think I know where you need to go to finish your quest, I haven't really taken notice of what you've said has been happening around me as long as I had a good surf each day and fish to eat I was content but from what you said that is all going to change. At that Andysurf went out of the cabin asking Dick and Tom to come out too, once they were all standing on the beach Andysurf pointed down the beach saying around that corner in the next cove you will find a dark cave anything that goes in that cove never returns and if they do they look different but not in a good way. Both boys looked to Andysurf and then to each other Dick saying well we now have a good idea where we need to go but what about our horses we won't need to take them with us we will be able to walk there which may be for the best, Andysurf said not a problem your horses can stay here I'll take care of them, okay great said Tom lets go.

The boys set off down the beach and around to the cove Andysurf had told them about as they got closer it got darker the area getting grey and as they got to the front of the cave everything was black so black in the cave the boys couldn't see anything, Dick looked at Tom saying I think this is the right place it's not just dark its cold yes said Tom, They drew their swords out and put their shields on their arms as they stepped into the entrance of the cave they're swords started to glow lighting their way, Wow said Tom this must be because Sparagus polished them with the porridge, Dick nodded shushing Tom.

As they crept further into the cave their glowing swords in front of them they could hear creepy singing and laughing as they went in further they came upon a cavern and in the middle of this

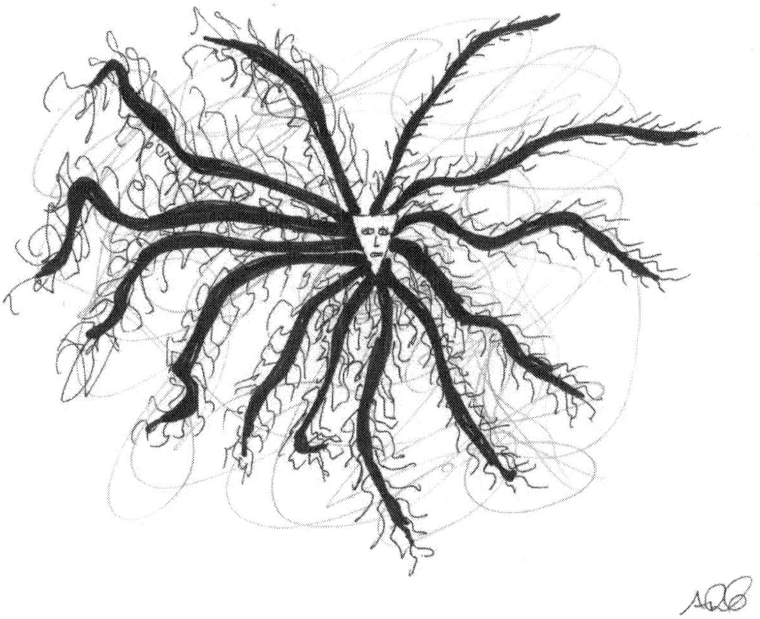

cavern was a hideous thing it looked like a spider but it had 13 legs and a triangular head with eyes a nose and mouth and the hideous noises were coming from that mouth she was suspended on a web like structure as they got closer it stopped singing and laughing and said well hello Prince Dick and Knight Tom I have been waiting for you as you Prince Dick is the final piece to my winning and then started laughing again, Dick said why do you need me and as he said that he ran forward swinging his sword at the things legs but as he hit two another two swung out knocking him to the ground holding him there, Tom ran to other side to do the same but again she used her other legs to knock Tom to the ground holding him down. My name is Nightshade and I am going to destroy this realm all I need is the curse I placed in you Dick to succeed at that is to take it from you she placed her arm closest to her head on Dick closed her eyes and started chanting, all of a sudden she screamed throwing both boys away from her saying what have you done it's not there where is it I need it, while Nightshade was distracted the boys noticed a gulley running under her they nodded at each other put their shields on the floor at the beginning of the gulley then jumped on their shields like a surf board and rode them under Nightshade as they went under they raised their swords yelling as they went Nightshade looked down to see what was happening and the boys were able to cut off her head, they carried on down the gulley coming out of the back of the cave onto a beach, and standing on that beach was all the friends they'd made along the way, their parents and even better the sky was blue as was the sea the sand was yellow and the plants were green and the flowers full off colour .

Everyone was shouting and laughing hugging each other and Dick and Tom, they finally got to their parents saying how did you get and even more important how did you know we would succeed, Dicks father the King spoke for them all when he said Jakelm came and got us bringing us here as for knowing you would succeed the stranger told us plus we knew your hearts would not let you fail, Now let's celebrate color and laughter in this realm.

The party went on for a long time Dick and Tom decided to go for a walk to gather their thoughts wondering what happens next, as they walked along they suddenly came across a strange man sitting on the beach they went up to him asking are you alright, yes of course I am hello Dick, Tom my name is Emeris, what but that makes you the stranger said Dick looking around them the boys asked what he was doing there, to which he replied I am here to say well done and to answer your question of what happens next, oh well your welcome the boys said and what does happen next, to which Emeris said you will return with your parents to where you were raised carrying on your lives as if none of this happened and no not because you won't remember but because you are needed there for now but don't worry you will return here again, Dick and Tom looked at each other but when they looked back to ask Emeris what he meant he was gone.

The boys went back to the party and when the coach turned up and their parents said its time to go home the boys got in without arguing giving Jakelm and Peony a hug goodbye whispering in Peony's ear till the next time.

Goodbye everyone till the boys return in the search for Peony.

Printed in Great Britain
by Amazon